D1053107

Mostly Monty

Johanna Hurwitz

illustrated by
Anik McGrory

CANDLEWICK PRESS
CAMBRIDGE, MASSACHUSETTS

Mostly for Fiona, Juliet, & Ethan
J. H.

Mostly for Monica
A. M.

Text copyright © 2007 by Johanna Hurwitz
Illustrations copyright © 2007 by Anik McGrory

First edition 2007

Library of Congress Cataloging-in-Publication Data
Hurwitz, Johanna
Mostly Monty / Johanna Hurwitz ; illustrated by Anik McGrory. —1st ed.
p.   cm.
Summary: Because he suffers from asthma, six-year-old Monty
is nervous about starting first grade but he soon learns to cope
with his illness and use his special talents to make friends.
ISBN 978-0-7636-2831-4
[1. Asthma—Fiction. 2. Schools—Fiction.]
I. McGrory, Anik, ill. II. Title.
PZ7.H9574Mos 2007
[E]—dc22   2006049024

2 4 6 8 10 9 7 5 3 1

Printed in the United States of America

This book was typeset in Stempel Schneidler.
The illustrations were done in watercolor.

Candlewick Press
2067 Massachusetts Avenue
Cambridge, Massachusetts 02140

visit us at www.candlewick.com

Contents

✿

1

Meet Monty

This is what Montgomery Gerald Morris had:

A nickname: Monty.

A birthday on August 15. This year he had turned six.

Asthma, which sometimes made it difficult for him to breathe.

An inhaler. It was made of plastic and contained medicine. He carried it in his pocket wherever he went. If he felt that an asthma attack was coming on, he pulled it out real fast and put it in his mouth.

This is what Monty didn't have:

A brother or a sister.

A pet.

Monty also didn't have a best friend.

He didn't have any real friends at all.

It was no wonder. Because of his asthma,

he wasn't permitted to go running around outdoors like other kids. He couldn't join the Little League team. He couldn't plan to go to sleepaway camp when he got older. Who would want to be friends with a boy like him?

Monty's parents were very protective of their son. They worried about his health. Twice in the past, he'd wakened in the night unable to breathe. Both times, he had been rushed to the hospital. It sounds exciting to ride off in an ambulance with a siren and blinking lights. For Monty, it hadn't been exciting at all. It was scary. Monty didn't complain about his limitations, but he didn't like them either. Why did he have to have asthma anyhow?

Now Monty was in first grade. Before school started, he had been very nervous. Staying at school all day seemed like a long time to be away from home. Even having his own packed lunch with a sandwich and drink, a piece of fruit, and a treat wasn't enough to make

Monty glad to be in first grade. He was used to eating lunch at the kitchen table in his own house. So on the first day of first grade, he felt scared. He sat quietly in his seat while many of his classmates chattered together. He recognized a few faces from kindergarten, but there were many new faces too. He put his hand in his pants pocket to feel for his inhaler. It was good to know that it was handy if he had an asthma attack.

On that first morning, the teacher clapped her hands for attention. "My name is Mrs. Meaney," she announced to the students.

Monty shuddered. *Mrs. Meaney.* That sounded as if she would be a mean teacher. He glanced around to see if the other boys and girls in his class were worried about that too. Everyone sat at attention looking at the teacher, so it was hard to tell.

For the rest of the day and the days that followed, Monty sat quietly in his first-grade classroom, answering questions only when he had to. Usually he just watched everyone else. Even at lunchtime, he sat quietly chewing his sandwich and watching the other students. He tried to imagine what it would be like to be Gregory Lawson, who could run faster than anyone in the whole grade. He wondered what it felt like to be

Joey Thomas, who lived down his street and owned not one but two dogs, which he walked every day after school. And he tried to imagine being his classmate Ilene Kelly, who had a twin sister named Arlene in a different section of first grade. The Kelly sisters lived down the street from Monty too.

It seemed to Monty that it would be more fun and more interesting to be someone else.

He didn't enjoy being Monty at all.

There was one good thing, however. It turned out that Mrs. Meaney wasn't mean at all. She smiled a lot. She didn't scold when the students talked with one another when they should have been doing their work. And she didn't shout—even when she saw Paul Freeman drawing on his arm with a blue marker.

"What are you doing?" she asked Paul.

"I'm making a tattoo," Paul responded.

"A tattoo? What in the world do you need a tattoo for?" she asked him.

Monty looked at his classmate in amazement. No one should write on their skin. They should write on paper. Somehow, Paul hadn't learned that in kindergarten. Monty would never do anything as silly as that.

On Friday of the first week of first grade, Monty began to have trouble breathing. He dropped his pencil and grabbed his inhaler out of his pocket. He put it in his mouth and breathed deeply. Of course, the kids sitting near him noticed at once.

"What is that?" asked Cindy Green.

"Is it something to eat?" asked Paul Freeman.

Monty didn't answer. He just shook his head and continued breathing deeply. He was relieved when Mrs. Meaney came over. She told the students to pay attention to their workbooks and not to Monty. Then she asked Cora Rose to accompany Monty to the nurse's office.

"Do you feel horrible?" asked Cora Rose. She had been in Monty's kindergarten class last year.

Monty shook his head. Actually, he was feeling much better already.

"Do you think you are going to die?" asked Cora Rose.

"Of course," Monty responded, taking the inhaler away from his mouth. "Everyone is going to die someday. But not for a long, long, long time. Don't you remember how our class rabbit died last year when we were in kindergarten? Everyone's got to die sometime."

"Me too?" asked Cora Rose.

"You too," Monty told her. Then he felt sorry that he had said anything. Cora Rose began to look upset. In fact, she started to cry.

At that moment, they reached the nurse's office. The nurse's name was Mrs. Lamb.

"Good morning," she greeted the two first-graders. She looked at Cora Rose. "Don't you feel well?" she asked her. "Where does it hurt you, honey?"

"Monty says I'm going to die," Cora Rose reported, sniffing back her tears.

"But I told her not for a long, long, long time," Monty protested.

It took a couple of minutes for Mrs. Lamb to sort it all out. Cora Rose was not sick. And by now, neither was Monty. His slight asthma attack had passed. Mrs. Lamb assured them that they were both healthy and going to live for a long, long, long time. Then the two students returned to their class.

Later that same day, when the children were taking turns reading aloud, Mrs. Meaney complimented Monty on his reading ability. "You are an excellent reader," she told him. "I'll have to find a more difficult book for you."

Monty beamed with pride. He had learned to read all by himself during the summer.

He looked forward to the following week, when the class was scheduled to go to the school library. Last year, when the students were in kindergarten, they went once a week to hear stories. This year, they would hear stories, and they could borrow books to take home too. Monty loved reading, and he was looking forward to this new privilege.

A week later, when they went to the library, Mr. Harris, the school librarian, showed the students where the picture books were shelved. "This is the section where you will find the books for your age," he told the first-graders. "You may even recognize some of the stories that I've read to you. Today you can take one home and ask your parents to read it to you."

At once, the students began looking through the books. Not Monty. He didn't want a storybook with pictures. He wanted a book with lots of information in it. During the summer, when he went to the public library, he had learned about the special numbers on the information books that arranged them by subject. He knew where to find science books, so this was a chance to pick out one of those. Mr. Harris didn't say the students must borrow a storybook, but he hadn't said anything about looking at the other books. Timidly, Monty walked across the room.

He looked for the books about animals in the 500 section of the shelves.

Mr. Harris saw him and came over. "I don't think you'll like these," he said. "They are much too difficult for a first-grader. They'll be waiting for you in a couple of years when you can read them."

Monty swallowed hard. He took a deep breath and reached for the inhaler in his pocket just in case he needed it. He felt his eyes filling with tears. He didn't want to cry like a baby, but he knew he could read these hard books. Reading was one thing he could do without worrying about his breathing.

Luckily, at that moment, Mrs. Meaney came over to them. "Monty is a wonderful reader. I think he could read almost any book he wants to," she told the librarian.

"Really?" asked Mr. Harris. "Good for you, Monty. You're my kind of guy. Just show me what you want before you check it out."

Monty smiled at both his teacher and the librarian. Mrs. Meaney patted him on the shoulder. "Are you interested in anything special?" she asked. "Sharks, dinosaurs, planets, or something like that?"

"I'm interested in everything," said Monty softly.

"Great," said Mrs. Meaney. "That's wonderful. Just look around, then. And if you need assistance, either Mr. Harris or I will help you."

Monty picked out a large book filled with pictures and information about dinosaurs. Next time, he might get a book about New York City. That's where his mother had lived when she was his age. He thought it would be interesting to learn more about it.

When the first-graders lined up to check out their books, Mr. Harris nodded his approval of Monty's choice. But Joey Thomas, who was standing in line behind Monty, shook his head. "You can't read that book. It's too big. And it will be too hard."

Once again, Monty swallowed hard. He took a deep breath and blinked back the tears that he felt forming in his eyes. Even though Joey lived on his street, the two boys never played together.

But Ilene Kelly, who was standing in front of Monty, spoke to Joey. "You're just jealous," she said to him. She looked at Monty. "I heard Mrs. Meaney say you're a good reader," she told him.

"That's right," agreed Cora Rose, who was standing in front of Ilene.

Monty knew the girls were right. He was a good reader. He was probably the best reader in his class. When the students read aloud, he'd heard the others stumble over words that he thought were very easy. He smiled at Ilene and Cora. It was nice of them to defend him. But he wished that he was good at something else, like running or playing soccer or making friends. He looked down at his library book. He looked forward to reading it at home, but he still wished he was someone else and not Monty.

2

What Monty Got

One day, the first-graders talked about their pets. Mrs. Meaney said they would write stories about them. Only three children in the class didn't have pets, and of course, Monty was one of them. "You can write about a pet you would like to have," Mrs. Meaney told the three petless students.

Monty really wished he had a pet. His first choice would have been a dog. Second choice was a cat. Third was a guinea pig. Fourth was a hamster. His choices grew smaller and smaller, but his mother's response was louder and louder. "No dog, no cat. No guinea pig. No hamster. All those animals are out," she told him. "Animal hair will give you an asthma attack. I'm sorry, Monty," she said. "How about some goldfish? They don't have hair." But you can't cuddle a goldfish. In fact, you'd get wet when you even tried to touch a fish. So Monty turned that offer down.

Even though his mother had said no to all the animals that he suggested, Monty kept thinking about getting a pet.

"A baby kitten is very, very small," said Monty. "It wouldn't have much hair."

"A baby kitten would grow into a cat before long, and it would have lots of hair," his mother reminded him. And then before Monty could begin begging once again for a guinea pig or a hamster—a pet that would start out small and never grow big—she said, "It doesn't take much hair to start an asthma attack. Your father and I don't want you to have trouble breathing."

"If hair gives me an asthma attack, how come I'm not allergic to you or Dad?" asked Monty.

"That's a good question," said Monty's mom. "The next time we see the doctor, we'll have to ask him. Maybe he knows the answer."

So Monty wrote a report about a pet dinosaur.

"Nobody can have a pet dinosaur," said Joey Thomas when Monty read his report aloud in class.

"If I'm writing about a pretend pet, I guess it can be anything I want," said Monty.

Mrs. Meaney agreed. *Great job!* she wrote on Monty's paper. She drew a little smiley face on the paper too.

■ ■ ■

One afternoon, when Monty was playing in front of his house, he noticed something crawling on the sidewalk. It was a green caterpillar with a few black hairs sticking out of its body. He stopped to watch it. Then he picked it up. He thought he'd put the caterpillar on a bush so no one would step on it. Then he had a better idea. He put it on his arm. He watched as the caterpillar moved its small head around and then slowly began walking up his sleeve.

Monty bent his head down close to the caterpillar and took a deep breath. Nothing happened. At once, he felt a glow of delight. It appeared that he was not allergic to caterpillars. He watched as the caterpillar slowly moved up his arm.

"I bet you think my arm is a mountain," Monty whispered to the caterpillar.

Of course, the caterpillar could not respond. It just kept moving slowly upward.

When the caterpillar reached his shoulder, Monty picked it up and put it back down by his wrist. Once again, the caterpillar began its mountain climb. Walking carefully so as not to disturb the small creature that was climbing up his arm, Monty went into the house.

"Mom!" he shouted to his mother. "I have a pet!"

Mrs. Morris came running from the kitchen. She saw the green caterpillar just as it was once again about to reach her son's shoulder.

"Is that your pet?" she asked with relief.

"Yes. It's okay if I keep it, isn't it?" asked Monty. "I'm not allergic to caterpillars. It hardly has any hairs at all."

"Of course you can keep it," said Monty's mom. "Let me see what we can put it in."

Monty followed his mother into the kitchen. From the cupboard she took an empty mayonnaise jar. "I think this will make a good home," said Mrs. Morris.

"I'm going to put some twigs and leaves inside the jar," said Monty excitedly. "It will make my caterpillar feel more like he's still outdoors."

"Good idea," agreed Mrs. Morris. "Let's see if I can make some holes in the lid so there will be enough air for the caterpillar to breathe."

Monty named the caterpillar Charlie. That night, Charlie slept inside his new home. At his dad's suggestion, Monty had put a bottle cap with fresh water into the jar in case Charlie got thirsty during the night.

Monty realized that as pets go, Charlie was awfully small. He couldn't pet him much either because his parents thought it might disturb the caterpillar. Still, there was something special about him. Maybe it was because Monty had discovered Charlie by himself, or maybe it was because he had given him a name.

At school the next day, he told Mrs. Meaney that he had a new pet. She seemed surprised when she heard that Charlie was a green caterpillar with black hairs. And it was Monty who was surprised when he came home from school one day to discover that Charlie was beginning to build a cocoon around himself.

Monty checked on Charlie every morning when he woke up, then again after school, and again before bedtime. Soon he couldn't see Charlie because he was hidden inside the cocoon. "I bet it's nice and cozy in there," Monty told his parents. Unfortunately, Charlie wasn't very interesting to watch now that he was inside the cocoon.

Then one morning several weeks later, Monty noticed that the cocoon was open. On the bottom of the jar was a moth with pale yellow wings.

He ran with the jar into the kitchen to show his parents this new development. They were both surprised. Then Monty's dad said, "You know, Monty, moths and butterflies have wings so they can fly. Don't you think you should let Charlie use those new wings of his?"

"You mean let him go?" asked Monty.

Mr. Morris nodded.

Monty studied the creature inside the jar. The wings moved slightly as he watched.

"If I had wings, I'd want to fly," said Monty with a sigh. "I guess Charlie should fly too." He started to open the jar.

"Wait! Not in the house," said his mother. "You can open the jar just before you go to school."

Monty put the jar on the kitchen table and went back into his bedroom. He was still wearing his pajamas, so he had to get dressed. Then he returned to the kitchen and had his breakfast: corn flakes with milk and sliced banana.

All the time he was eating, he watched the new Charlie. He would be a little bit sad to let him go, he thought. But he knew it was the right thing to do.

Monty's parents stood next to him as he took the jar outside. He removed the lid. Monty waited, but Charlie didn't fly out.

"Maybe Charlie wants to stay with me, even if he can fly away," said Monty hopefully.

"Maybe he's not quite ready to go yet," said Monty's mom. "But it's time for you to leave for school. So let's just rest the open jar on this window ledge."

That seemed like a good plan. "Good-bye, Charlie," Monty called as he picked up his backpack. "Maybe I'll see you this afternoon."

"And maybe you won't," said Monty's dad. "If he's gone, you'll know he's off having a good time using his new wings."

As it turned out, Charlie was not in the jar when Monty returned home from school.

But Monty wasn't too sad about it. He thought that if he watched carefully, he might get to see Charlie flying by one day soon. He had another thought too. If he kept his eyes open, he was almost sure to find another caterpillar, which could move into the vacant jar at his house.

3

What Monty Saw

One Saturday morning, when Monty was outside searching for another caterpillar, he saw a huge pile of items sitting at the end of the driveway next door. There was an old chair with a cane bottom that had a hole in it, two old suitcases, a huge stack of old magazines, some old flowerpots, and a red wagon—except it was so rusty that in some places there was no paint on it at all. Monty admired the wagon. It might come in useful, he thought. Everything piled up the way it was made it appear as if his neighbor Mrs. Carlton might be waiting for the trash collectors. Monty decided to find out for sure.

He rang the doorbell.

"Why, hello, Monty," exclaimed Mrs. Carlton. "I'm afraid I won't be your neighbor much longer. But I will certainly miss your infectious smile."

Infectious! Monty felt his face turning red. Did Mrs. Carlton think she could catch his asthma and get sick too? Asthma was not that kind of sickness. It was a little like the birthmark his classmate Ethan had on his eyelid. It was something he was born with.

"You don't have to move away. I'm not infectious. You won't get sick from me," Monty insisted.

For a moment, Mrs. Carlton looked puzzled. Then she realized why Monty was concerned. "Of course I won't get sick from you," said his neighbor, giving Monty a hug. "When I said your smile was infectious, I meant that the smile is catching. When I see you smiling, it makes me want to do the same thing."

Monty smiled at his neighbor and she smiled back at him.

"Why are you moving away?" he asked.

"I've decided this place is too big for me. And I want to move closer to my son and his family. So I'm clearing out the house, and then I'm putting it up for sale."

"Does that mean you don't want the wagon and the other stuff that's outside?" Monty asked.

"It certainly does. The wagon belonged to my son when he was your age. Now he's forty years old. That wagon is almost an antique."

"Can I have it?" asked Monty.

"Of course," his neighbor said. "In fact, come in and look around. Maybe there's something else here that you want. I haven't taken everything outside yet. It's going to take me a long time to clear it all out."

Monty went into Mrs. Carlton's house. He'd been there before. Sometimes when his mother baked cookies or made a big pot of soup, she'd send Monty over with some as a gift. Once, he'd gone over and borrowed two eggs from Mrs. Carlton when his mother discovered that she didn't have enough for the recipe she was preparing.

"Look at this," said Mrs. Carlton.

Monty saw some boxes of puzzles, a pile of books, and an old teddy bear with a friendly smile. "Jeffrey told me last night to just throw it all out. For years, he insisted that I keep every single thing for his children. But now he says they've outgrown all this stuff," said Mrs. Carlton.

Monty took everything. He took the puzzles, the books, and even the old teddy

bear. It took three trips in and out of the house to fill the old wagon with all these new possessions. It was like finding hidden treasure, he thought happily. He pulled the wagon carefully toward home. He noticed that one of the wheels was wobbly. Maybe his dad could help him fix it, he thought.

"Look what I've got," said Monty proudly to his parents.

"Wow!" exclaimed Mr. Morris, looking at all the stuff Monty had. "I think you hit the jackpot."

Monty nodded happily.

"I guess you'd better count the pieces before you start putting any of those puzzles together. It would be terrible to put in a lot of work only to discover that you were missing a few important bits and couldn't finish it," said Mr. Morris.

"Good idea," said Monty's mom. "Let me smell that bear," she said, looking at the teddy bear that Monty had brought home in the wagon.

"Smell it?" asked Monty. It had never occurred to him to do that.

Because of his asthma, his parents had made a point of not giving him stuffed toys when he was little. They worried that the lint they contained would not be good for him.

"Sometimes old stuffed toys get musty or moldy," his mother explained. She picked up the bear and gave a sniff.

"Just as I thought," she said, nodding. "I'm afraid this fellow has seen better days. He belongs in the trash."

"That's where he was going when I got him," said Monty. "Can't we put him in the washing machine? Maybe he'll smell better then."

"I'll throw him in the next dark wash and we'll see what happens," his mother agreed. "He is a cute fellow. They did a much nicer job of making teddy bears in the old days," she said, admiring the toy. "But aren't you too old for stuffed animals?"

Monty thought for a moment. Was a first-grade boy too grown up for a teddy bear?

"Oh, no," he said. "I like him. He has such a friendly face. And I always wanted a teddy bear."

"What are those books?" Mr. Morris asked with interest. "Books are good even if they are old. And you certainly like to read," he said, smiling at his son.

But a closer inspection of the books showed that they weren't so good after all. Several of them were geography books that had been old even when Mrs. Carlton's son was a boy. "Most of the countries in Africa have the wrong names," said Mr. Morris as he flipped through the pages of one of the books. There was a science book, and it opened to a page that read, *Someday, in the distant future, it's possible that man will walk on the moon.*

"Uh-oh. That's very old," said Mrs. Morris. "The first man walked on the moon back in 1969. A good story can never become out of date, but an old nonfiction book can be filled with misinformation."

"I guess I'll put these books out with our garbage," said Monty, sighing.

He looked at the first puzzle box. On the lid was a picture of an aquarium filled with many colorful fish. The box said 200 Pieces. That would be fun to do. Monty dumped the pieces out and began counting. The total came to only 187 pieces. Hoping he'd made a mistake, he counted again, and got only 185. "This has to go in the trash too," he said sorrowfully.

He checked the pieces in the other boxes. None of them was complete.

"At least I got a new wagon. Or a new old wagon," he told his parents. He gave the wagon a little pull, and the wobbly wheel stopped being wobbly. It fell off the wagon altogether.

"Oh, dear, I'm afraid this is beyond repair," said Mr. Morris, inspecting the wagon. "The screws are all rusty, and so are the holes where new ones would go. I'm sorry," he told his son. "Maybe we can get you a brand-new wagon with four good wheels for your birthday."

"Will it be red?" asked Monty hopefully.

"Of course," said his dad.

"When are you doing a wash?" Monty asked his mom. It looked as if all his newfound possessions were going out to the garbage. And it was a long way off till his next birthday. But maybe they could still rescue the teddy bear.

"I'll do one now," said Mrs. Morris.

The large orange sanitation truck came while the teddy bear was still in the washing machine. The broken chair and the suitcases and the old magazines in front of Mrs. Carlton's house were picked up. The old books, the puzzles with the missing pieces, and the rusty wagon with three attached wheels and one that had fallen off were picked up too.

At last, the spin cycle of the washing machine was completed, and the teddy bear was taken out, together with the clothing he had been washed with.

"I'll put him in the dryer for a little while," said Mrs. Morris.

Monty went down to the basement and watched the teddy bear spinning around inside the dryer. He hoped when it finished spinning, the bear would smell good.

Finally, the buzzer went off. It meant the drying was completed. Mrs. Morris removed the dark clothing and the teddy bear from the machine. She sniffed at the bear and smiled. "What do you think?" she asked Monty.

Monty took a deep breath. "He smells good," he said happily.

So even though he didn't get any new books or puzzles or a wagon that day, Monty did get the teddy bear with the friendly smile. It sat on his bed, smelling good. And that night, it slept inside the bed, with Monty. Just looking at it made Monty feel good too.

4

What Monty Found

Not everything Monty saw lying around belonged in the garbage. One Monday just as recess was ending, Monty found a sweater lying in a corner of the playground. It was dark gray and it was near a gray wall, so it would have been easy to miss. In fact, it had been missed by its owner, which is why Monty found it.

On his way back to his classroom, he stopped in the school office and handed the sweater to Mrs. Remsen, the secretary. Under her desk was a carton labeled LOST & FOUND.

"I found this," he informed her.

Mrs. Remsen took her eyeglasses off the top of her head, where she often left them, and, putting them on, she examined the sweater. "There's no nametape sewn inside," she commented. "There's no brand label either. This is a hand-knit sweater, and someone put a lot of work into making it. I hope the owner has enough sense to come looking." Then she turned to Monty and smiled at him. "Thanks for being such a good citizen," she told him.

Monty blushed. He could go for days without anyone noticing him. It wasn't often that someone at school praised him. So he felt very good, even if he was embarrassed at the same time.

After that, Monty spent a lot of time looking for lost items around the school. Some of them he knew would never be claimed: a chewed pencil, a red mitten with a hole in it, a notebook with its cover torn off. Still, he took them to the office. He liked showing what a good finder he was, even when the stuff he found wasn't very important. But then the following week, he made several important finds: a pair of boots, a book from the public library, a Yankees baseball cap, and a dollar bill. He thought about keeping the dollar. No one would know if he did. All dollars look the same. Still, he felt he had a responsibility to turn in every lost item that he found.

"Monty, you're amazing," said Mrs. Remsen when he turned up for the fourth day in a row. "I'm going to call you Mr. Lost and Found from now on."

Monty blushed with pleasure. He liked Mrs. Remsen, and when she smiled at him, he could see that she liked him too.

"I can't believe how careless some of the students are with their property," the secretary said to him. "If they weren't attached, I'm sure you'd be finding lost heads rolling around the hallways."

Monty laughed aloud at Mrs. Remsen's words.

"Maybe I'll find a head tomorrow," he said, joking back.

"Well, keep up the good work," the secretary told him.

After four days of finding lost possessions, Monty did not find anything the next day, which was Friday. He wondered if people were more careful on Fridays.

When he returned to school after the weekend, Monty looked hard to find something. But there was nothing on the playground, nothing in the lunchroom, and nothing in the boys' room, waiting for him to find it. He didn't find anything on Tuesday or Wednesday either. By Thursday, Monty thought that Mrs. Remsen would never call him Mr. Lost and Found again.

On Friday, Monty noticed a library book sticking out of Cora Rose's desk, and he thought about taking it and bringing it to the Lost and Found. The book wasn't exactly lost, but if he took it and turned it in, then it would be lost. When Cora noticed it was gone, he could tell her to check in the front office, and then the book would be found. But while he was thinking all this through, Cora, who had been off in the girls' room, returned to her seat. So the whole plan was no longer possible.

Then Monty had another idea. He could take something of his own and bring it to Mrs. Remsen. He considered what he had with him: his backpack, his jacket, his baseball cap, his wristwatch, and his lunch bag.

He remembered that his mother had sewn nametapes into his jacket and cap. She had written his name on the inside of the backpack in indelible ink. There were no identifying marks on his wristwatch, but he couldn't bear to be parted from it. That left only his lunch bag.

Monty had eaten a bigger breakfast than usual. He'd had some scrambled eggs with a slice of whole wheat toast, a glass of orange juice, and a glass of milk. He didn't feel the least bit hungry. He wouldn't need any lunch at all.

He raised his hand. Mrs. Meaney called on him.

"Can I take this lunch bag that I found down to the office?" he asked his teacher. It wasn't a lie at all. He had found the lunch bag. He'd found it on the counter in the kitchen at home.

"Of course," Mrs. Meaney said.

Monty took the bag and hurried toward the school office. He looked it over as he

went to double-check that his name wasn't
on it. Wouldn't it be awful if he gave the bag
to Mrs. Remsen and she knew it was not
really lost at all?

The brown paper bag looked just like a hundred other bags in kids' backpacks. Reassured, Monty walked into the office with it.

Mrs. Remsen looked up from some writing that she was doing. "Don't tell me you found that lunch?" she said.

Monty nodded.

"Lunches never go into the Lost and Found box," the secretary told him. "They begin to smell after a few hours. I'll leave it right here on my desk. Hopefully the owner will realize it's missing and come and get it."

Monty nodded again even though he knew that was not going to happen. He would never come back and admit it was his lunch on Mrs. Remsen's desk.

As he turned to go, the secretary called out to him. "By the way, Monty," she said, "no one came looking for a dollar bill all week, so I think you should take this now." She reached into the Lost and Found box and pulled out the money.

"Wow! Thanks," said Monty. He put the dollar deep into his pants pocket. He certainly didn't want to lose it, like its original owner had. He wondered what he should spend it on.

"No. Thank *you* for being such a responsible citizen," Mrs. Remsen insisted.

Monty returned to class feeling very good. In fact, he felt so good about himself that he raised his hand and answered a question that he thought he knew the answer to but wasn't a hundred percent sure. On any other day, he would have let someone else answer. As it happened, he was right, so that made him feel even better. It was turning out to be a wonderful day.

By lunchtime, Monty was feeling very hungry. He couldn't wait to see what his mother had given him for lunch. He pulled open his backpack to get his bag, then remembered that his lunch wasn't there. It was sitting on Mrs. Remsen's desk.

There was no way that Monty was going to retrieve it. Instead, he followed his classmates to the lunchroom. There was so much coming and going and talking and laughing that no one even seemed to notice that Monty didn't have any lunch. If they saw he wasn't eating, they may have decided that he'd already finished his lunch or else that he hadn't started yet. No one noticed but Monty's stomach. It complained to him as if it hadn't been given a good breakfast this morning and a perfectly good supper the night before.

Just when Monty thought he might faint from hunger, he remembered the dollar bill in his pocket.

He rushed over to the lunch line and discovered that he had enough money for a bowl of vegetable soup with crackers and also an apple and a container of milk. He ate every bite and drank every drop.

When the kids went outside for recess, he ran along with them. He looked around, but he didn't find anything lost that day. So he sat on a step near the door to the school, and he thought about how he would spend the dollar that Mrs. Remsen had given him. He was really lucky to have this money. It would be enough for a—

Suddenly it occurred to Monty that he no longer had the dollar. He hadn't exactly lost it, like the kid who had it before him. But by spending it at lunchtime, he'd lost the chance to spend it on something else. How could he have been so stupid? The more he thought about it, the more Monty realized he'd been silly to hand over his lunch to the Lost and Found. It was a perfectly good meal that had been wasted.

He got up and walked around the

playground. It occurred to him if he had found a dollar bill once, it was possible that he'd find another one. In fact, next time he might even find a five-dollar bill. If he did, he'd certainly be much more careful with it.

When the bell rang for the students to go back inside, Monty discovered that he'd almost forgotten his jacket. Luckily he found it—just where he'd left it, on the step. That was good luck. It wouldn't be right for Mr. Lost and Found to start losing things.

5

What Monty Did

In class one day, Mrs. Meaney talked about
hobbies. "Hobbies are activities that give you
pleasure and keep you busy," she told the
students. Very few of the first graders had
hobbies. But Cora Rose said she liked to help
her mother cook. Mrs. Meaney said cooking
was a good hobby.

"My hobby is watching TV," said Paul Freeman.

"Watching television is fun, but it's not a good hobby," Mrs. Meaney told him. "You need a hobby that will keep your brain busy."

"TV keeps my brain busy," Paul insisted.

"I play on the computer," said someone else.

"That's good," said Mrs. Meaney. "Some people also like to collect things for a hobby." The students talked about the types of things that people collected: stamps, coins, postcards, and other things that could be pasted into albums or scrapbooks.

Monty wanted a hobby, but he didn't want to paste anything into an album. He wanted a different kind of activity. It would be fun to have a hobby to do while he wasn't in school. Of course, Monty liked to read.

It was the one activity that he could do really well. In fact, Mrs. Meaney had reported to his parents that he read on a fourth-grade level. But he was still in first grade and he needed a first-grade activity to keep him busy.

After school one Friday, while Monty was reading a book about Australia, he got an idea.

"I have a hobby," he announced to his parents that evening during supper.

"What is it?" his mother asked.

Monty had a big smile on his face as he told them.

"Kangaroos," he said.

"What kind of a hobby is that?" asked his mother with amazement.

"It's *my* hobby," said Monty.

"That's great," said his father. "But you can't collect them. You can't paste them into an album like stamps. What will you do?"

"I can read about them. I can study all the books in the library and look on the Internet and become an expert on the subject," said Monty. "Soon I'll know more about kangaroos than anyone around here."

"That shouldn't be very hard," said his father.

"I'm starting right after supper," said Monty, and he did.

First he went to the computer and typed in the word *kangaroos* on a search engine, the way he'd been taught at school. Soon he began printing out information. There were many pictures of the animals, so that gave him an idea. "I can make a scrapbook of kangaroo pictures," he called to his parents.

Now that he had a hobby, the idea of pasting
pictures began to interest him.

Then Monty had another idea. "I'm going
to start a kangaroo club," he told them.

"With kangaroos? There aren't any
kangaroos around here," his father said.

"Not *with* kangaroos," said Monty. "*About* kangaroos." It was amazing what little imagination his parents seemed to have.

"Clubs need members," Monty's mother said.

"Sure. But first I need rules," Monty responded.

He made a list:

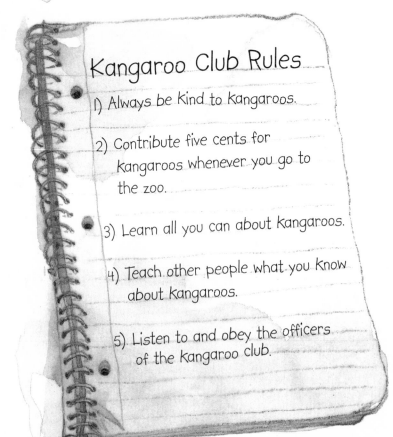

Kangaroo Club Rules

1) Always be kind to kangaroos.

2) Contribute five cents for kangaroos whenever you go to the zoo.

3) Learn all you can about kangaroos.

4) Teach other people what you know about kangaroos.

5) Listen to and obey the officers of the kangaroo club.

Monty's mother looked over his shoulder. "Who are the officers of the club?" she asked.

"So far there is only a president," said Monty. "I am the president," he told her proudly.

"Who will be vice president?" asked his father.

"The next person who joins the club will be the vice president. Would you like to join?"

Mr. Morris scratched his head. "That's a nice offer," he told his son, "but I think you should find some members who are closer to your age. What do you think? Aren't there other kids around here who might also like kangaroos?"

"Everyone would like kangaroos if they knew more about them," said Monty.

He realized he had a big job cut out for

himself. He had to teach other kids about kangaroos. Then they would want to join his club. He'd been thinking about Joey Thomas, who lived down the street. Even though they lived on the same street and were in the same class, the two boys had never become friends. Still, Joey had two dogs, so that showed he liked animals. Monty thought Joey might be interested when he learned that a baby kangaroo was called a *joey*. In fact, Joey Thomas might think that was reason enough for him to become president of the club. But after all, the club was Monty's idea. So he would remain president. He printed up a sheet of kangaroo facts to give his neighbor the next day.

When Monty saw Joey Thomas walking down the street with his two dogs, he ran after him. He didn't have to worry about dog hair outdoors. It was only inside a house that the hair might bother his asthma. Still, before he began speaking, he put his hand in his pocket and held on to his inhaler for support.

"Do you want to join a club?" Monty asked Joey.

"What kind of club?" Joey asked.

"A kangaroo club," said Monty. He began to explain his plan.

Joey listened to Monty. He looked at the sheet of kangaroo information that Monty held up.

"This is just like school," Joey complained. "You shouldn't have to read this kind of stuff if it isn't homework. Especially when it's the weekend," he added. One of Joey's dogs pulled on his leash.

"Down, Jupiter!" shouted Joey.

The dog sat down. Monty was impressed.

"Kangaroos are very interesting," Monty said.

Joey studied the sheet of paper. This is what it said:

Kangaroos come in different sizes.

The littlest weigh one pound. The biggest weigh 175 pounds.

They have pouches for holding their babies.

A little kangaroo is called a joey.

They're great at hopping.

Their tails help them keep their balance when they hop.

Kangaroos are vegetarian.

They live in Australia.

They also live in zoos.

"Where did you learn all this?" Joey asked. "I never knew my name was the same as a kangaroo."

"I've been reading about them," Monty explained. "If you join my club, we can learn more information. And my mom said she'd serve refreshments," he added.

"Ice cream?"

"Maybe, or cookies. Something different at each meeting, I guess," said Monty.

"How many meetings will there be?" asked Joey.

"It's a club. So we'll have to vote on it," Monty explained. "I'm the president, but you can be vice president."

Joey agreed to go to the first meeting of the Kangaroo Club at Monty's house that afternoon after lunch.

"Who else will be there?" Joey asked as he turned to go off with his dogs.

"You'll see at the meeting," Monty said. At that moment, he didn't know who else would be at the meeting himself.

"What's the name of your other dog?" he shouted to Joey.

"Pluto" was the reply.

That was a surprise to Monty. He hadn't known that his classmate was interested in astronomy.

Having gotten one new member, it was easier to get the others. The twins, Ilene, who was also in his class, and Arlene, lived at the other end of Monty's street. They said that they would come. Their little cousin Evan was visiting from out of town. Monty told Evan that he could join too. So that meant that five kids were sitting in the sun porch of Monty's house that afternoon for the very first meeting of the Kangaroo Club.

Monty gave out fact sheets about kangaroos for the members to study.

"Maybe we can take a trip to the zoo," suggested Ilene. "Then we can go and look at real kangaroos."

"That's a great idea," said Monty, beaming. "Do you think your mother would take us?"

"We can ask her," Ilene said. "She'll probably say yes because she wants Evan to have a good time while he's visiting. Maybe we can go tomorrow."

Evan was only four years old, and this was his first time away from home. "I like zoos," he said.

"Do we have to look only at kangaroos?" Joey asked.

"Let's vote on it," said Monty. "That's what clubs do."

"All in favor of just looking at kangaroos at the zoo, raise your hand," said Joey.

Monty raised his hand.

"All in favor of looking at all the other animals too, raise your hand," said Joey.

Five hands went up into the air—because Evan raised both of his.

"Okay. Other animals win," said Joey triumphantly.

"But we'll look at the kangaroos first," said Monty. "After all, this is the Kangaroo Club."

"That's fair," said Ilene. Arlene agreed.

They planned to meet every week. Each member would try to have a new kangaroo fact to share with the others at every meeting. Dues would be five cents. They would contribute that money to the zoo for the upkeep of the kangaroos. "It won't pay for much," said Joey.

"Kangaroos are cheap to take care of. Remember, they eat grass and leaves. No meat," said Monty.

At Arlene's suggestion, the five club members took turns hopping around the sun porch, pretending to be kangaroos. Despite being the youngest, Evan was an excellent hopper.

"Are you ready for refreshments?" asked Mrs. Morris, coming out onto the sun porch with a large tray in her hands.

She put the tray down. If Joey, Ilene, and Arlene had been wondering whether they were going to be served salad, which would be similar to kangaroos' food of grass and leaves, they needn't have worried. On the tray was a container of vanilla ice cream, with bowls and spoons for everyone. There was also a choice of butterscotch or fudge sauce.

"Ice cream sundaes!" shouted Joey with delight. "I like this club. Can we make a rule that we always have the same refreshments?"

Everyone turned to look at the club president. Monty doubted that his mother would agree to serving butterscotch and fudge sauce at each meeting. He thought quickly.

"My mom bakes very good cakes," he said.

"I vote that we be surprised each time," said Arlene.

"All in favor?"

Six hands went up. (Evan raised both of his.)

"Poor kangaroos. They never get to eat ice cream," said Ilene, licking butterscotch sauce off her fingers.

When the meeting of the Kangaroo Club was over for that day, Monty knew he'd found the best thing ever. He'd found three and a half new friends. (He only counted Evan as half a friend because he was so young and he'd be going home tomorrow evening.)

He helped his mother by drying the dishes from the club refreshments. Then he went to read one of his library books. Just before he started reading, he realized something.

He was feeling pretty good. It wasn't because his asthma hadn't bothered him in many weeks. It wasn't from eating ice cream with fudge sauce. It wasn't even from having new friends. It was mostly because he was glad to be himself. He liked being Monty after all.